charlie's
DIRT
DAY

Andrew Larsen

Illustrated by

Jacqueline Hudon-Verrelli

Fitzhenry & Whiteside

Published in Canada by Fitzhenry & Whiteside, 195 Allstate Parkway, Markham, ON, L3R 4T8
www.fitzhenry.ca
Published in the U.S. by Fitzhenry & Whiteside, 311 Washington Street, Brighton, Massachusetts 02135

We acknowledge with thanks the Canada Council for the Arts, and the Ontario Arts Council for their support of our publishing program. We acknowledge the financial support of the Government of Canada through the Canada Book Fund (CBF) for our publishing activities.

Library and Archives Canada Cataloguing in Publication
ISBN 978-1-55455-334-1 (bound)
Data available on file

Publisher Cataloging-in-Publication Data (U.S.)
ISBN 978-1-55455-334-1 (bound)
Data available on file

Text and cover design by Daniel Choi
Cover illustration courtesy of Jacqueline Hudon-Verrelli

Printed and bound in China by Sheck Wah Tong Printing Press Ltd.

This story began as a tiny seed of an idea. That seed has been nurtured by many caring hands.
With thanks to Cathy, Christie, Jack, Wendy, Kathy, and Cheryl.

–A.L.

For my son, Félix.

–J.H-V

Charlie stands on his balcony.

He looks up.

Way up...

Clouds float.

Planes fly.

Birds soar.

The sky goes on and on and on.

He looks down....

Trees grow.

Cars slow.

The sidewalk goes on and on and on.

What on earth?

What is going on?

And on and on?

Nannies and grannies and moms and
dads and boys and girls and cats and
dogs and wagons and wheelbarrows
and buckets and bowls…and babies, too!

Phew!

They're all coming up the sidewalk.

"Dad!" Charlie calls out. "Come see! There's a parade passing by!"

"A parade?" says his dad, stepping onto the balcony.

"A parade!" says Charlie.

"I love a parade!" says his dad.

Nannies and grannies and moms and dads and boys and girls and cats and dogs and wagons and wheelbarrows and buckets and bowls and babies…and now Charlie and his dad, too!

Phew!

But where is everybody going?

And what are they doing?

Finally, the parade of people arrives at the park. And **there**, in the middle of the park, is a big pile of dirt.

A big pile of dirt? All this hullaballoo for a big pile of dirt?

"Step right up!" barks a man in a green uniform. "Welcome to the mayor's annual Dirt Day Giveaway. We've got free dirt for everyone."

"Free dirt?" says Charlie's dad. "Is that it? Dirt?"

"It's not just any old dirt," says the man in the green uniform. "It's the richest, dirtiest dirt you'll ever see. It's fresh compost. Your gardens will love it."

"Compost?" says Charlie. "What's that?"

"It's recycled kitchen and garden waste," says the man. "We use a special recipe to turn the old waste into something new and useful—something called compost. It's like magic. You put it back into the garden and it feeds everything that grows."

"I wish I had a garden," sighs Charlie.

"What are you going to do with all that compost?" Charlie asks Mr. Martino.

"I'll use most of it for the tomatoes in my garden," replies Mr. Martino. "Then I'll take some to Mrs. Lee for the onions she grows in her backyard. I'll give the rest to Mr. Patel for the herbs he grows on his balcony."

"On his balcony?" says Charlie. "Mr. Patel grows herbs on his balcony?"

"Lots of people grow lots of things on their balcony," says Mr. Martino. "A balcony is like a garden in the sky."

"At the end of the summer I'll up cook my tomatoes and I'll add some of Mrs. Lee's onions," continues Mr. Martino. "Then I'll flavour it with some of Mr. Patel's herbs. It's my own recipe. I call it *Martino's Marvellous Spaghetti Sauce.*"

"I love spaghetti!" says Charlie.

"Here," says the man in the green uniform, handing Charlie a little clay pot. "There's a seed in the soil. It'll need water and light. If you take care of it, it will grow."

"But I don't have a garden," worries Charlie.

"A window or a balcony will do," says the man.

Charlie cradles the pot in his arms.

"I'm going to take care of this seed," he says, "and it's going to grow big and strong."

Like all the other gardeners who have been to Dirt Day, Charlie leaves a tiny trail of dirt on his way home.

He puts the pot in
the window and gives
it a drink of water.

"There," he says.

He watches it.

And waits.…

Time passes…

and grows….

and the seed grows…

And Charlie?

He grows a little too.

Finally, it's time to harvest all the wonderful food that grew with a little help from the mayor's compost.

Mr. Martino invites Charlie to help him make his Marvellous Spaghetti Sauce.

He cooks up his tomatoes and adds some of Mrs. Lee's onions. He flavours it with some of Mr. Patel's herbs.

Then Charlie adds his own special ingredient.

Delicious!

The next year, on Dirt Day, Charlie and his dad join the parade again. They take their buckets and their shovels so that Charlie can make a garden on the balcony—his own garden in the sky.

Charlie wants to grow something new to add to Mr. Martino's Marvellous Spaghetti Sauce.

Garlic?

Chili Peppers?

Beans?

The possibilities are endless.

They grow on and on and on....

What's the Scoop on Dirt?

In *Charlie's Dirt Day*, the words dirt, soil and compost are used as if they mean the same thing. In fact, they mean very different things.

Dirt is the stuff we sweep away and clean. The most common type of dirt is dust, which is a powder made up of both organic and mineral matter.

Soil is alive! It's full of billions of tiny creatures that are invisible to the naked eye. It's the earth beneath our feet. Soil is a mixture of organic material (material that originates from living things, including plant and animal life), minerals, water, and air. Plants and trees need soil to grow and we need plants and trees to live.

Compost is the result of the amazing transformation of organic material into a substance that provides nutrients for plants. It is crumbly, dark, and earth-like. Compost improves the soil and helps plants to grow bigger and stronger.

Community Gardens

Community gardens are increasingly a part of city life. They are usually built on abandoned or underused land. They give many people, especially people who don't have their own gardens, a chance to become urban farmers in the company of their neighbours. Friendships and laughter grow alongside herbs and vegetables.

Tell Me More About Composting

Nature recycles leaves and plants so that, over time, they decompose or break down into nutrients that will benefit the soil. We can recycle too! Composting is an easy, effective, and environmentally friendly way of recycling organic materials such as food waste, newspaper, pet waste, garden waste, etc. into nutrient-rich food for gardens.

How Does Nature Compost?

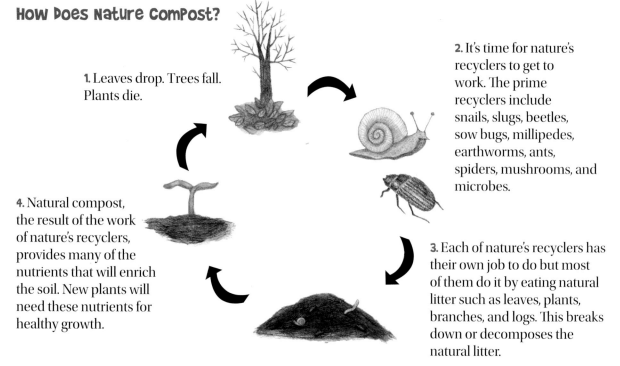

1. Leaves drop. Trees fall. Plants die.

2. It's time for nature's recyclers to get to work. The prime recyclers include snails, slugs, beetles, sow bugs, millipedes, earthworms, ants, spiders, mushrooms, and microbes.

3. Each of nature's recyclers has their own job to do but most of them do it by eating natural litter such as leaves, plants, branches, and logs. This breaks down or decomposes the natural litter.

4. Natural compost, the result of the work of nature's recyclers, provides many of the nutrients that will enrich the soil. New plants will need these nutrients for healthy growth.

How Do Towns Compost?

Many cities collect waste from kitchens and gardens separately from other types of garbage. The organic waste is brought to special processing facilities designed to encourage the natural process of decomposition. For example, some facilities shred and stir the organic waste while pumping air through it. This helps to speed up the process and makes it more efficient.

The compost produced in these facilities can be given back to the community (like in *Charlie's Dirt Day*) and can be put into gardens to make the soil strong. It's the circle of recycling.

How Can I Compost?

By separating organic kitchen and garden waste and putting it out on garbage day, you can do your part to recycle and compost. If you have a backyard you can compost your own organic waste in a bin or in a drum or in a pile.

Gardens in the Sky

The Fairmont Royal York Hotel in Toronto, Ontario has a 14th-floor rooftop garden. Herbs and vegetables, including sweet cherry tomatoes, thrive in specially constructed growing beds. Six beehives are home to over 300,000 bees. The bees produce up to 350 kilograms of honey per year. Even better, as the bees forage for nectar, they pollinate thousands of plants in the downtown core of Toronto. The herbs, vegetables, and honey are served in the hotel's restaurants.

If you'd like to have a garden in the sky, all you need is soil, sun, and some sort of container. Almost anything will do. Even a reusable grocery bag!

Here's the scoop on growing cherry tomatoes from seed:

1. Prepare a small pot with potting soil.
2. Poke a hole about 1/4 inch into the soil and place 2 or 3 seeds (available at your local gardening store or at most hardware stores) in the hole.
3. Cover the seeds with soil.
4. Place the pot in a window that gets plenty of sun and water the plants every day, just enough to keep the soil moist.
5. Watch the seeds grow into plants (4–6 weeks).
6. As the plants grow, they will have to be transferred into a larger container and moved to a sunny spot outside. This is because the roots of the plants will need room to grow.
7. Add a small amount of compost to nourish the growing cherry tomato plant.
8. Keep watering and watch the tomatoes grow.
9. Harvest your tomatoes like an urban farmer!

From the time you plant the seeds until the time you are able to harvest the cherry tomatoes will be about 2 to 3 months. Herbs, peas, and beans can be grown and harvested in much less time.

Wiggly Worms

Worms love to tunnel. Their tunnels loosen the soil. This allows air and water to enter the soil and keep it healthy.

Worms also love to eat. Their appetite is an important element in nature's recycling process. A worm can eat its own weight in organic matter each and every day.

Although you might think it's gross, people in many countries eat worms because of their abundance and their high nutritional value.

Compost in a Cup

You can make your own compost.

You'll need:

- Organic compostable items: leaves, vegetable scraps, fruit scraps, coffee grinds, egg shells, etc.—no meat or dairy
- 1/4 cup soil
- 1–2 teaspoons of water
- Large bowl
- Large spoon
- 16-oz. plastic cup with tiny holes in the bottom
- Piece of plastic wrap and a rubber band
- Saucer

1. Place the organic items in a large bowl, add 1/4 cup of soil and 1–2 teaspoons of water. Stir with a large spoon.
2. Using the spoon, take 2 scoops from the bowl and place them into your cup.
3. Place plastic wrap on top of the cup and secure with a rubber band.
4. Put the cup on the saucer to collect liquids that drain from the bottom.
5. Put the saucer by a window so that it gets sun during the day.
6. Once every few days, add a teaspoon of water to the cup and give the contents a little shake to help with the composting process.
7. Watch as nature slowly does its thing and creates compost.

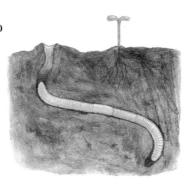